The Spider-
Slayer

Graham Marks

To Becs!

At Last!

![signature]

▣ *sapling*

First published in Great Britain in 1995 by Sapling, an imprint of
Boxtree Limited, Broadwall House, 21 Broadwall, London SE1 9PL

ISBN: 0 7522 0147 6

A CIP catalogue entry for this book is available from the British
Library.

Typeset by SX Composing, Rayleigh, Essex
Printed and bound in Great Britain by Cox & Wyman, Reading,
Berkshire.

Chapter One

'It's nice just to get away up here sometimes,' thought Spider-Man, as he landed neatly on the side of an office building. He stayed still for a moment, enjoying the quiet of the night, but then suddenly his eyes narrowed. Peering into the pitch blackness of the cloudless night sky he could see five lights hanging in the air. He stared hard, finally making out the small insect-like shapes beneath the lights, picking up the hum of their wings.

'What are they?' Spider-Man muttered to himself as he

1

watched them watching him. And then one of the insects made a swift darting move. 'Looks nasty, whatever it is.' Dodging sideways, Spider-Man did a handspring up the building, twisting almost faster than the eye could see.

But not so fast that a camera couldn't record it. In a room in a building somewhere in New York city, a man watched, fascinated, as the screens in front of him showed pictures of Spider-Man trying to evade the Seekers.

'His speed . . . his sheer *agility*!' said a very English voice. 'It's amazing!'

*

Seconds later Spider-Man was on the rooftop. And there was something buzzing close behind him. Spinning round, he saw a black metallic insect rise above the roof wall and turn his way. Luckily for Spider-Man, it went too close to the wall. One of its wings clipped the brickwork and a split second later the thing was spinning out of control over his head and crashing into the roof.

It exploded and the blast knocked him off his feet. 'Bet you don't come with a no-quibble guarantee!' He grinned, and then saw a second machine coming straight for him. 'Time for some *serious* action,' he said grimly.

Spider-Man lassoed the on-coming machine, slung it around his head and let go. Swiftly reaching for his belt, he grabbed his camera and took pictures as the machine crashed into a billboard and exploded in a ball of flame.

In the silence that followed, he heard an insistent buzzing and looked round to see two more of the robotic insects. 'Playing cow-boys was OK,' he said, swinging down, 'but follow-the-leader's going to be better!'

Spider-Man suddenly turned sharp right into a narrow street. A quick glance over his shoulder told him that only one of the machines was following. 'It's an old trick,' he said to himself, spotting the second machine coming from the other end of the street, 'but this time it's not going to work!'

He let go of the web, dropping like a stone, and above him the two robots ploughed into each other, disintegrating in a bright orange fireball. Picking himself up, Spider-Man dazedly shook his head, trying to get rid of yet more buzzing.

'Well, hello, Number Five,' he said, webbing the last of the flying robots and pulling it down sharply. As it hit the street, it blew up. 'So who's on my tail *this* time?' he wondered out loud.

*

In the room in the building somewhere in New York city, the video-screens suddenly went blank and then faded back with nothing but an electronic snowstorm.

'You blew it!' said a gruff voice. 'I don't appreciate failure, Smythe!'

'My father is the world's foremost expert in robotics, Mr Osborn,' said Alistair Smythe from his wheelchair. 'He is *not* a failure.'

'Relax, Alistair,' said Spencer Smythe. 'You don't have to defend me.'

'He doesn't?' said Normon Osborn, President of Oscorp, in

mock surprise. 'You let that web-swinging weasel make fools of us!'

'This was only a test run,' explained Spencer. 'The Spider-Seekers have proved that my targeting software can find Spider-Man.'

'*My* targeting software and Seekers,' interrupted Osborn. 'You invented them with Oscorp's money – and what good are they if they can't actually catch him?'

'That's not their job,' said Spencer.

'Then whose job is it, pray tell?' said Osborn raising a sarcastic eyebrow.

Spencer didn't react. Instead he opened one of the panels in the room. '*That*'s whose job it is,' he said, pointing at the half-completed skeleton of a huge spider-like robot. 'Gentlemen, I give you my Spider-Slayer – the Black Widow!'

Chapter Two

Peter Parker was in the *Daily Bugle* newsroom, checking his pictures of the flying robots. He was pleased – considering the conditions under which they'd been taken – but now he was lost in thought over his latest assignment. He was to act as official photographer at the Charity Ball being hosted that evening by his boss, J. Jonah Jameson, and the mother of his beautiful classmate Felicia Hardy.

'Parker! Why are you still here?' Jameson's voice echoed round the newsroom and brought Peter right back down to earth. 'Haven't you got work to do? And where's Eddie Brock? Wasn't he supposed to have some big scoop for me?'

Putting the photographs in the Picture Editor's in-tray, Peter grabbed his camera bag and left the office, wondering if he'd get to dance with the gorgeous Felicia at the ball.

'You won't regret bringing me in on this, Mr Smythe,' said Eddie Brock, the *Bugle*'s star reporter, as he watched the finishing touches being made to the Spider-Slayer. 'It'll be my biggest story yet – the capture of Spider-Man!'

'You're here as insurance,' said

Spencer, 'to see things don't get out of hand.'

'I don't intend to harm the man,' growled Osborn. 'I just want him behind bars!'

'Some news story!' grinned Brock. 'But I've got to go now. See you all later!'

'I've an appointment myself,' said Osborn, following Brock to the door. 'You have to trust me, Smythe. Everything'll be done by the book.'

'I *never* trust anyone who says I *have* to trust him,' said Alistair, as the door closed.

'I have my reasons,' said his father, wheeling him over to a holo-projector and turning it on.

The 3D image of a cybernetic hover-chair sprang into being. 'As I'm sure you can now understand.'

'Our getting Spider-Man is paying for this?' Alistair pointed at the hologram.

'The explosion which put you in that wheelchair was my fault,' said Spencer, frowning. 'I'd do *anything* to make amends.'

'Even work with a creep like Osborn?'

'He's not *that* bad, Alistair . . .'

Crime Central, the heart of the Kingpin's criminal empire, was on top of a massive skyscraper. Information from around the globe was fed into this villainous nerve centre, giving the crime-lord a complete picture of his worldwide business. And this was where Osborn had his appointment.

'The Black Widow's ready,' he said as he walked into the room.

'Does anyone suspect my involvement?' asked the Kingpin, a huge, dark shape sitting in shadow at his desk.

'No one.'

'Good. That's just as it should be.' He sat forward, his face coming into the light. 'My livelihood is continually being threatened by the sudden and unwanted appearance of that costumed do-gooder. How does it look to the rest of the world if I can't control my own home town because of one measly super hero?'

'The Black Widow can neutralize Spider-Man's powers,' said Osborn. 'You have nothing to worry about."

'But you do, Osborn. If you fail, I get control of Oscorp.'

'Either way, you win,' said Osborn.

'But of course!' laughed the big man. 'That's why *I'm* the Kingpin!'

The Charity Ball was in full swing when Peter Parker arrived. He'd brought his widowed Aunt May with him, whom he lived with. The moment she saw them, Felicia Hardy left her boyfriend, Peter's none-too-bright classmate Flash Thompson, to come and say hello. This did nothing to change Flash's opinion of 'Bookworm' Parker. He'd never liked him and was always on the look-out for ways to make him appear stupid.

'Harry,' he said to his companion, the heir to the Oscorp millions, 'I think it's time to put our little plan into action!'

'What d'you think Parker will do when he sees you in your Spidey costume, Flash?' grinned Harry.

'Hopefully make a complete idiot of himself!' Flash laughed.

As the two of them left the ball to get the costume from Flash's car, a Seeker sailed into view high above the building, its camera searching for a certain wall-crawling super hero.

Chapter Three

'Got him!' crowed Spencer.

Alistair Smythe watched his father excitedly pointing at the grainy picture of Spider-Man, and wondered whether they were doing the right thing. But it was too late to stop now, because Stage Two of the operation was already in progress.

'He's at 39th and Second,' Spencer continued.

'That's Jameson's place – where he's having the Charity Ball!' Brock clapped his hands. 'The boss is going to have a front-row seat!'

'Good for him,' growled Osborn. 'Now, can we get this show on the road?'

Spencer looked at his wheelchair-bound son, took a deep breath and activated the Spider-Slayer. Clouds of smoke billowed out as the roof of the lab opened and the Black Widow jetted into the night sky with one thought in its silicon mind: *Get Spider-Man!*

Peter was in seventh heaven – he was actually *waltzing* with Felicia Hardy. And then suddenly his spider-sense started tingling. 'Why *now*?' he whispered under his breath. 'What could possibly happen here?'

Voices around the room started to yell and the music came to a ragged halt. Through the crowds, Peter could see someone in a very familiar red and blue costume.

'Why is *he* here?' asked Felicia in a small, fearful voice.

'It's some kind of joke,' said Peter, grinning, and he patted her arm comfortingly as he started walking towards the fake Spider-Man.

'Parker!' said the impostor, grabbing Peter's dinner jacket. 'I don't like those pictures you keep taking of me and I want an apolo – *Geez!* What the heck's *that*?'

Peter looked behind him at

where the impostor was pointing and saw a squat, black insectoid robot fly in through the open doorway that led to the balcony.

The fake Spider-Man let go of Peter and ran for it, then tripped, fell and disappeared under a stampede of guests. Peter left Felicia and dashed over to where Aunt May was standing. He hustled her into what turned out to be a large bedroom and closed the door. Then, looking round, he spotted a dark alcove and, seconds later, reappeared in full costume to find the penthouse in uproar.

He leapt up, clinging to the ceiling. Beneath him he could see the spider-like robot clanking across the room. 'Hey, you!' he yelled. 'Your name wasn't on the guest list!'

The machine stopped and looked upwards. Spider-Man dropped down and, in one fluid move, launched himself at the Slayer, bouncing off its armoured shell.

'A tougher nut than I thought,' he said, picking himself up as one of the robot's servo-arms made a vicious swipe. A swift backflip took him well out of its reach. Scanning the room, Spider-Man saw that the impostor appeared to have gone, along with most of the guests . . . And then he spotted

Felicia.

She'd run between him and the robot and was screaming hysterically at it. Spider-Man grabbed a red tablecloth from the floor and waved it, toreador-style, to attract the Slayer's attention. As a ploy it worked only too well. The Black Widow immediately turned from Felicia and made straight for him, crashing into a steel beam supporting the penthouse roof.

Spider-Man desperately tried to hold the roof up. For a moment he thought he could do it, but then there was an almighty crack and the roof gave way, dust and rubble hitting the carpet like heavy rain, taking Spider-Man with it.

The Black Widow advanced through the thick cloud of debris, its high-resolution camera on full gain, searching for its prey. It stopped in front of a semi-conscious blue and red form on the floor and picked it up. Then its jets roared into life and it soared out of the devastated penthouse.

Chapter Four

Surrounded by what was now a million-dollar rubbish heap, J. Jonah Jameson watched as the emergency services milled around the smoking ruins. From somewhere he could hear the sound of a TV set, and it appeared to be coming from the master bedroom.

'Here is the moment the whole US of A has been waiting for!' said a voice that Jameson immediately recognized – it was Eddie Brock. *'The unmasking of Spider-Man!'*

'So that's what Brock's big scoop was all about!' yelled Jameson as he opened the door. Suddenly noticing the little old lady watching TV, he turned to her. 'Excuse me, are you all right, ma'am?'

'Just fine,' said Aunt May, eyes glued to the set.

'*And now, live and exclusively . . .*' Brock was saying, as he reached out and pulled the mask off.

'Flash Thompson?' said an amazed Aunt May. 'But he goes to college with my nephew!'

'You're telling me Spider-Man's some overgrown *school*kid?' howled Jameson. 'That's un-believable!'

'No more than your supposed income-tax returns, J. J.,' said a voice from the ceiling.

'*There you have it, America – the face of a super-criminal,*' Brock went on, as Jameson stared up at the face of . . . Spider-Man! He was speechless. How could the web-slinging hero be in two places at once?

'*Any minute now,*' continued Brock, '*the police will be here to arrest . . .*' He stopped and looked out of camera shot. '*I can't believe it!*' he continued. '*Some people have broken into the Oscorp labs and . . . What do you want?*'

'*Him!*' said a masked man, pointing a high-tech laser pistol at Flash Thompson. And then he slammed it into the camera, turning the picture on Jameson's TV to static.

'That Thompson boy's in big trouble. Someone should try and save him!' said Aunt May, looking up at the ceiling. But now there was no one there.

'OK, let's finish up here,' said the leader of the team of masked men, pointing his laser pistol at the now conscious Flash. 'Otherwise the Kingpin'll finish *us* off.'

'The Kingpin?' frowned Spencer, looking over at Osborn.

'Spencer, I swear – ' Osborn cringed. 'This wasn't the plan!'

'Wrong,' said the masked man. He was about to fire when he heard a disturbance outside the heavily guarded room.

'No!' wailed Flash, as the door to the room burst open. 'You don't understand – please!'

A stream of web-line hit the laser. 'He *said* "please" – ' Spider-Man caught the pistol as it whipped back to him – 'so killing the guy's *not* a very nice thing to do.'

'*Two* of 'em?' said the gang leader, confused.

'Terrific, you can count!' Spider-Man leapt towards him, and the man guarding Flash joined in the fight. In all the confusion, Flash managed to crawl from the room, past the gang members Spider-Man had knocked out, and run off up some stairs.

'Turn the Black Widow on

again!' a guard ordered Spencer.

'No way!' he scowled. The man pointed his laser at Alistair. 'Very well, . . . *that* button.'

The masked man punched the control panel and the robot made straight for Spider-Man. With a graceful punch-kick combo, he laid out the two men attacking him, picked up a heavy steel rod and faced the advancing machine.

An already dangerous situation soon got much worse. The duo Spider-Man had knocked out came to and began firing. Then Osborn leant over and activated a Seeker. Hitting the Widow with the pole, Spider-Man webbed the two men, spun round and swung the steel rod at the Seeker. It connected with a satisfying crunch and sent the tiny flyer smashing into a wall, where it burst into flame.

In the middle of all the chaos, Brock and Spencer, who was pushing Alistair, made for the nearest door.

'Remember our deal, Smythe?' said Osborn, grabbing Spencer's arm. 'No Spider-Man, no hover-chair.'

Spencer hesitated, looking at his son. 'All right,' he said finally, 'but take Alistair out of here.' Without a backward glance as Brock and Osborn pushed the wheelchair away, Spencer ran back to the Slayer's control panel.

Spider-Man is confronted by Spencer Smythe's robotic 'insects'.

Spidey gets ready for some serious action with the Seekers.

Peter Parker has quite a surprise from Felicia Hardy . . .

The Spider-Slayer embarks on its mission to catch Spider-Man and leaves a trail of destruction at the Charity Ball.

The
Spider-
Slayer
launches
at
Spidey
crushing
him to
the
ground
with one
strong
blow.

Flash
Thompson
regrets
imitating a
superhero
– he's no
match for
the Spider-
Slayer!

With three deadly powers at the Spider-Slayers' control panel, Spider-Man has a fight on his hands!

Alistair looks in horror as Oscorp is destroyed. Will he carry on his father's work?

Chapter Five

With Spencer now controlling his master-creation, the Black Widow tore the steel rod out of Spider-Man's hands and then chased after him as he leapt up a towering column that ran centrally through the Oscorp lab.

Ripping pieces of piping from the column as he climbed, Spider-Man flung them behind him in an effort to slow the Widow down. But even though he managed to dislodge its feet, sending it tumbling into space, all the robot did was go into jet mode and fly straight back at him.

Spider-Man was still in front when the Widow shot out a stream of slippery oil into his path, and the next thing he knew, *he* was the one plummeting downwards, with nothing between him and oblivion but a killer robot.

Far below, Spencer was following events via the Slayer's camera. He saw Spider-Man slip and fall; he saw the camera turn to follow his death-plunge . . . but then there was nothing! It took a second for Spencer to realize what must have happened, and quickly he tapped the keyboard in front of him.

'You don't get rid of me *that* easily!' yelled Spider-Man, gripping more tightly on to the back of the Slayer as it bucked and spun. Whirling like some maddened bug, the Black Widow's video-lens suddenly caught a glimpse of red and blue amongst the pipework it was passing. The tracking software kicked into life and the Widow zoomed in on . . . Flash, hiding where he thought he'd never be found!

Trembling with fear, Flash screamed at the flying nightmare careening towards him, 'No! No! I'm not the one you want!'

'That's my boy,' grunted Spider-Man, pulling webbing cartridges off his belt. 'A picture of true grit.'

The Widow slowed and pulled

itself on to a metal catwalk that led to where Flash was cowering. Keeping out of range of the robot's camera, Spider-Man bent down and stuffed cartridges into each of its jet ports and then jumped off.

He could hear Flash babbling in pure panic as the Widow approached. He waited for just the right moment and then shot two webs at the machine's rear. He began to haul it backwards, closer and closer to the edge, until it lost its balance and fell. He watched it nosedive, and, right when he expected it, heard a couple of loud pops and saw the blocked jets blow. 'Worst case of heartburn I've ever seen,' he said, as the crippled Slayer spun uncontrollably to its doom.

Pulling the snivelling Flash out of his hiding place, Spider-Man looked down at him. 'Move it, buddy,' he said. 'We've got seconds before this whole place goes up!'

In the lab Spencer watched in utter dismay as the most perfect machine he'd ever built plunged directly into a massive vat of hyper-acid – the only thing that could completely destroy it! There was a splash, the sound of gruesome bubbling and then the whole building erupted in a deafening roar.

If anything, the dawn sun made the penthouse look even worse, and the sight had done nothing to calm J. Jonah Jameson's wicked temper as he yelled angrily at Eddie Brock. The whole *Bugle* organization had been humiliated by the events of the previous night, and Eddie was taking the full heat – in fact, he was getting fired.

Flash, still in what was left of his Spider-Man costume, was faring no better with Felicia, who couldn't believe he had pulled such an idiotic stunt at her mother's party. She had no more time for Peter either. After dropping Flash off, he'd changed and come back to get his aunt, only to find himself accused of cowardice for disappearing at the first sign of danger.

After a hard night, Peter hadn't the energy to do anything but go home.

Later, with wisps of smoke still rising from the wreckage, Alistair Smythe sat in his wheelchair and stared at what had once been the Oscorp lab – and was now his father's grave. A dark shadow loomed over him. 'A penny for your thoughts, Alistair?' said a deep, booming voice.

'You know me?' said Alistair, looking round at the huge man standing behind him.

'I was, how shall we say, an *associate* of your late father,' said the Kingpin. 'And now I want to be an associate of yours.'

'What good would that do me?'

'I could give you the money to build a new Black Widow,' the Kingpin said, smiling, 'and with it you can destroy the man responsible for your father's death: Spider-Man.'

Alistair thought for a moment and then gave a slight nod of his head. The deal had been struck.

Chapter Six

Some weeks later Spider-Man, out on one of his regular night patrols, was on a roof above the Empire State Building's observation deck. He'd just phoned Aunt May to try and get out of the blind date she'd finally managed to set up for him later that evening. He'd failed, and was wondering how bad Anna Watson's niece could be when his spider-sense started ringing alarm bells.

'Huh?' His eyes popped wide open, for coming towards him he could see . . . the Black Widow.

But the robot had been destroyed in this Oscorp lab!

Spider-Man blackflipped out of the way of two steel cables snaking towards him just as their rocket tips exploded the ledge he'd been on. 'A new, improved version,' he muttered, covering it with webbing – which it quickly sliced through.

Leaping up, Spider-Man grabbed a microwave relay dish and turned it on the Widow, frying its circuits. But his victory was short-lived. Over the roof clambered something looking just like a huge metallic tarantula, one of its massive legs tearing a radio mast loose and sending it crashing down.

The impact pitched Spider-Man off the roof – next stop, the pavement. He'd reached the seventh floor before he spotted a window-cleaning platform. His web caught it, jerking him to a halt, and he swung easily to the street. 'One day,' he said to himself, 'my luck's going to run out . . .'

He looked up and saw that the Widow had recovered from its microwaving and had joined the second robot in the chase. They were only five floors above him.

The Tarantula leapt from the building and landed in the street, its legs making deep holes in the tarmac. Spider-Man looped some web across the road and swung over the robot, dropping one of his tracers on its back before he alighted on the building opposite.

'I could get *really* fed up with this,' he said, jumping to the ground a second before a missile from the Tarantula shattered the sill he'd been standing on – only to find the Widow directly in front of him. 'Spiders, spiders everywhere!' he said.

In a high-tech laboratory, taking up the two floors above the Kingpin's Crime Central HQ, Alistair Smythe sat in his new eight-legged Personal Conveyor and watched the fight between

Spider-Man and two of his latest Slayers on the video-screen in front of him. He was controlling both robots through the alpha-wave transmitter on his head.

'Is that wall-crawler still alive?' enquired a voice from the shadows.

'Not for long, Kingpin,' replied Alistair, annoyed at the inter-ruption. 'Everything's going according to plan. He can't hold out for much longer.'

'Promises, promises. You'd better deliver . . . I'm rather *hard* on employees who fail me.'

'You'll soon have Spider-Man,' said Alistair, concentrating, 'and *I'll* have my revenge for what he did to my father!'

Back on the street, Spider-Man skidded to a halt as a puppy ran out of a building between him and the advancing Black Widow. A bad enough situation made even worse when its owner, a little girl, came after it, followed by her mother.

Hardly stopping to think, Spider-Man slung a line of web up to the top of a lamppost and swung over the Widow. Curving through the night air, he landed and gently pushed the terrified family off the street. Then he whirled round to face the enemy. 'Let's keep this just between us, shall we?'

He was concentrating so hard

on what the Slayer in front of him was doing that he failed to pick up the movement behind him until it was too late. The Tarantula's pulse-cannon blast hit Spider-Man in the back and, as he hit the pavement, the Widow snaked a couple of cables out and wrapped them round him.

'The old "Double Whammy",' thought Spider-Man, groggily trying to free himself. 'Dumb of me to let *that* happen.'

He just had time to plant a tracer on the Widow's steel tentacles as the Tarantula delivered its knock-out below – a gas grenade. The fight was over, but was the battle lost?

Chapter Seven

Spider-Man awoke to find himself handcuffed to, of all people, J. Jonah Jameson. The boss of the *Daily Bugle* was not a happy man. Alistair Smythe had tricked him into coming to his lab with the promise of being able, at last, to witness the capture of the person he hated most in the world. Instead he found himself attached to him by a pair of high-tech manacles.

'What are you doing?' yelled Jameson, looking down at the robot arm gripping his other wrist. 'I thought we had a deal.

What is this thing?'

'Titanium restraints . . . and a bomb,' said Alistair, smiling, 'which is set to detonate in exactly one hour.'

'Why are you doing this to *me*?' growled Jameson, tugging at the manacles.

'*Us*,' said Spider-Man. 'We both have ring-side seats for *this* show, J. J.'

'Because you're *both* re-sponsible for the death of my father.' Alistair punched the key-board in front of him. 'As are Flash Thompson, Eddie Brock and Norman Osborn. My Slayers are now programmed to take the two of you away and then set about destroying the other three!'

Alistair pressed a button and the Tarantula fired another gas grenade at Spider-Man and Jameson. 'Enjoy your sleep,' he said. 'It's the last you'll ever have.'

Jameson took longer to recover from the effects of the gas, so Spider-Man had to throw him over his shoulder and carry him down from the roof where the Tarantula had left them to die. He had less than an hour to find the others and warn them about Alistair Smythe's plans and to save them from the renewed threat of the Spider-slayers.

'Got the boss on my back *again*,'

he sighed as he swung away, following the spider-tracer he had placed on the Widow.

*

Outside the E.S.U. campus Student Union, Flash Thompson was trying hard not to say goodnight to Felicia Hardy. He was about to suggest they go somewhere for coffee when he heard a loud scream coming from a nearby building. Turning, he saw the ghastly robot Black Widow that had so nearly killed him only a few weeks before.

'Is this another of your stupid jokes, Flash?' asked Felicia.

'No!' yelled Flash, pushing her into the hall doorway as the

Widow spat a jet of acid at them –
which missed and melted the
wall.

With the Widow in hot pursuit,
Flash ran for his life. He fell to the
ground as one of the Widow's
steel cables wrapped itself round
his ankles and began to reel him
in. The Widow unsheathed two
vicious laser fangs, ready to
chomp on Flash, but instead the
deadly cutters sliced through . . .
a pair of titanium manacles!

Spider-Man leapt back as the
light-blades finished their job –
freeing Jameson, but leaving
Spidey with the bomb still on his
wrist. 'Now *that's* what I call
timing!' he said. 'Why don't you

guys go and make some phone calls while I deal with this beefed-up bug?'

The Widow was momentarily confused. It looked at the two people running away, which gave Spider-Man the chance to web the hook on a nearby crane in a building site, pull it down and attach it to one of the robot's legs.

As the Widow tried to move, Spider-Man webbed the crane's cab, swung up and started the motor. 'Don't have a licence to drive one of these,' he said, hauling the robot off the ground and slamming it into a wall until it stopped moving. 'And I keep on crashing into things . . .'

While Spider-Man was blitzing the Widow, Jameson was in a nearby phone booth. He'd spoken to his Editor, Robbie, and ordered a news team to cover the campus story. He'd warned Norman Osborn but he couldn't get hold of Eddie Brock.

Chapter Eight

Eddie had just been hired by the Editor of a rival newspaper when the Tarantula crashed through the roof of the newsroom and fired its pulse cannon at him.

'Why me?' screamed Brock, running from the office and exiting on to the street a moment later. The Tarantula followed down the wall of the newspaper building, blasting indiscriminately with its cannon.

Swatting a police car out of the way, the Tarantula stomped after Brock . . . and then he wasn't there any more. He'd been scooped up by a passing Spider-Man!

Swinging back to the pavement, Spider-Man dropped Brock by the newspaper office and turned to deal with the advancing Tarantula as it raised itself up on its four back legs. 'Must be my lucky day,' he said, grabbing one of the legs the Slayer was attempting to stab him with. 'I save Eddie and *still* have time to get blown up!'

Brutally twisting the Tarantula's leg, Spider-Man jammed it into the electrical supply box on the wall next to him and jumped back as high-voltage current zapped its circuitry.

'Shocking behaviour on my

part,' he said, swinging away, 'but there you go.'

The last person on Alistair Smythe's list was staring at a bank of video-screens. Norman Osborn was holed up inside his heavily fortified headquarters, satisfied that nothing could touch him.

But he hadn't reckoned on Alistair's crowning glory – the Scorpion! With a missile-tipped tail, plasma cannons and huge front claws, it was the deadliest of all the Slayers . . . and it was right outside the Oscorp gates. Osborn's satisfaction turned to sheer panic as he watched the lethal Slayer destroy almost a whole squadron of his compact robotanks and stomp towards the entrance.

'So little time, so much to do . . .', said Spider-Man. On the roof of the Oscorp building he nodded to himself, looking from the bomb on his wrist to the Scorpion down below. He swung away.

'Your machines have failed!' thundered the Kingpin, looking over Alistair's shoulder at the video-screens in front of him.

'Not yet . . . I'm activating reserve power packs in the Tarantula and the Widow.' Punching the keyboard, he watched the two robots come back to life and fly away. 'As soon as they link up with the Scorpion, there'll be a Tri-Spider-Slayer to deal with!'

Through narrowed eyes Spider-Man watched in disbelief as the Scorpion was joined by its two companions. 'If Smythe designed cars, they'd *never* break down,' he muttered.

No matter how hard the Oscorp security forces tried, they couldn't stop the Tri-Spider-Slayer. It ploughed through everything they threw in its path and was making short work of turning the main building to rubble. And that's when both the Tri-Spider-Slayer and Spider-Man spotted a car fish-tailing like crazy as it accelerated out of a side entrance.

'Osborn, making a getaway!' Spider-Man said, as he glanced at the bomb's timer. 'And it looks like bits of me might get there before him if I don't get this off soon . . .' It was then that he noticed the leaking liquid oxygen tank. Running over to it, he let some sub-zero fluid run over the manacles, cracking the metal and enabling him to free his wrist.

The Tri-Spider-Slayer robot had already taken off after Osborn. Picking up the bomb, Spider-Man pulled Osborn out of the front seat and up one of the towers just before the car exploded.

Hurling himself forward in a mad dash against time, Spider-Man eventually spotted the car. Osborn had made it half-way across the Brooklyn Bridge before crashing into the Tri-Spider-Slayer, which had landed in front of him. With plasma-cannon blasts erupting all around him, Spider-Man pulled Osborn out of the front seat and up on to one of the towers just before the car exploded.

'Hope you don't mind loud noises,' he said to the by now unconscious Osborn, 'because this gizmo of Smythe's is about to go critical!' He tied some webbing to the bomb and lobbed it at the Slayer. It jammed in the robot's uplifted claw. Spider-Man counted down the moments, then *boom!* – it blew up, and what was left of the evil invention that was supposed to be the end of Spider-Man fell into the river below, taking with it Alistair Smythe's dreams of revenge and the Kingpin's hopes of destroying his most hated foe.

'What a night!' sighed Peter, showered, changed and once more in the privacy of his room at Aunt May's. 'I've been battered, bruised and, to top it all, my costume's a mess.'

There was a knock at the door. 'Peter, dear,' said his aunt, 'I hope you're getting ready for your date with Mary Jane Watson tonight.'

'My blind date – what a perfect end to a *perfect* day!' Peter opened the door and stuck his head out. 'I'm not feeling too well, Aunt May, . . .' he said.

'But she'll be here any minute,' said Aunt May as the bell rang downstairs. 'That's her now. You'd better go and answer the door, Peter.'

'Don't I even get a last meal?' he muttered to himself as he turned the handle and opened the door. Nothing had prepared him for what he saw standing outside. He stopped dead in his tracks, his mouth open; waiting for him was the most stunning girl he'd *ever* seen.

'Face it, tiger,' smiled Mary Jane, 'you just hit the jackpot!'